'We're going to build a dam –

a big, strong dam.'

'We're going to dam a stream.

Hold its water back.'

For Ruari, son of one Calum
and Archie, son of the other Calum

First published in 2013 by Plaister Press
10 9 8 7 6 5 4 3 2 1

Copyright © Gillian McClure, 2013
The moral right of the author / illustrator has been asserted.

A CIP catalogue record for this book is available from
the British Library

Design: Lisa Kirkham

Printed in China

plaisterpress

Plaister Press Ltd
Registered address:
3 King Street
Castle Hedingham
Halstead
Essex
CO9 3ER
UK
www.plaisterpress.com

We're Going to Build a Dam

Gillian McClure

plaisterpress

Two boys go down
to the long, sandy beach,

where streams flow down to the sea

and a dog comes too.

'Have to find a stream.'

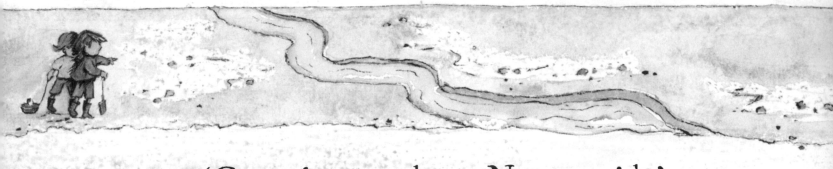

'Got to be a good one. Not too wide.'

'Not too fast.'

Two boys search the beach among
the rocks and dunes.

'Look!
Here's a nice, small one.'

'Got a shingle bed and sand banks.'

'Just the right stream to dam.'

Two boys survey the stream

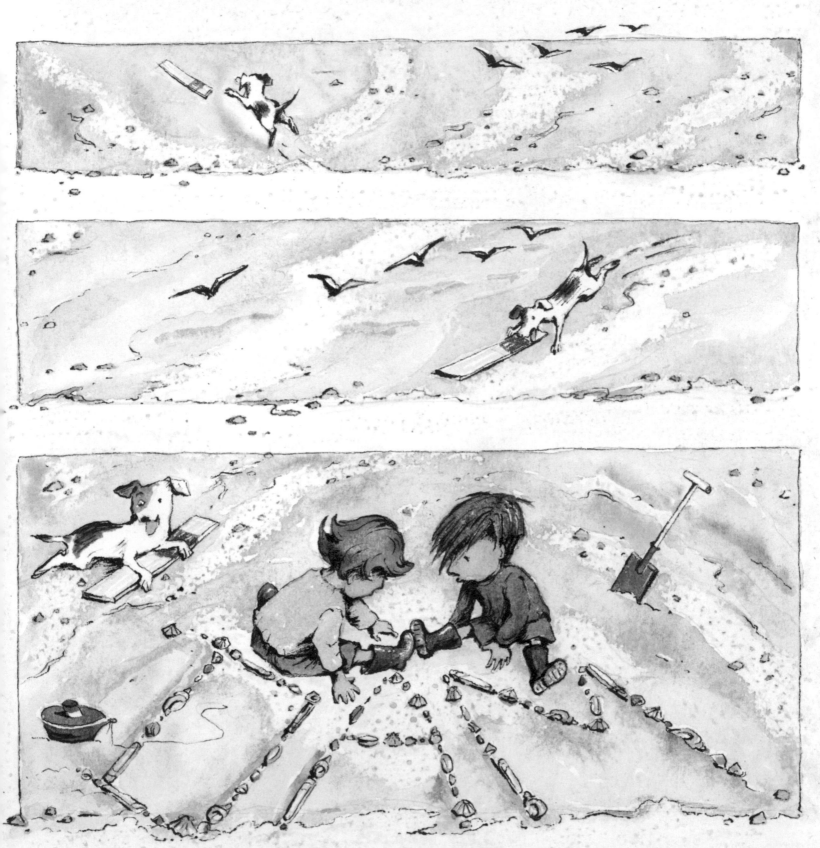

and draw up a plan in the sand.

'Dams are made of metal,
bricks and concrete blocks.'

'But we can do it
with beach stuff –

boulders

sand

and

rocks.'

Two boys roll a boulder
into the path of the stream.

'The stream's a cunning monster – it's flowing round the boulder, trying to get away.

What can we do to stop it?'

'Wedge in bits of driftwood.

Pad it out with sand bricks.

Coat it all with dribble sand.'

One boy picks up driftwood.

The other works
with sand.

'Stream's getting rattled. Hear it gurgle and growl. It's smashing against the driftwood that's standing in its way.'

'Weave in strands of seaweed. Tie it together like string.
Build out towards the boulder in the middle of the stream.'

'Stream's going mad. It's looking for a fight.
Coming like a BATTERING ram.
CRASHING against the dam.'

'QUICK! Fill the holes with pebbles.
Patch the gaps with grit.
Make the two sides meet.'

Two boys reach the boulder
and stop the last of the leaks.

The stream

BATTERS

The dam

SHUDDERS.

Will it hold?

All goes hushed and silent.

'Stream's given up.'

Two boys take a look ...

Above the dam,
water starts to spread.

Below, there's just a trickle
on the bare shingle bed.

'We did it!'

'We've held the water back.'

Two boys **Shout** and **cheer.**

Water rushes through –

popping out

pebbles

spitting stones and grit

Untying seaweed,

setting loose driftwood,

washing away sand bricks,

ROARING over the boulder, BREAKING down the dam.

Two boys stand and stare.
There's nothing they can do.

The dam's gone.
There's nothing left

but a small stream rippling round a boulder

and flowing on down to the sea.

Two boys walk back across the beach,
water in their wellies,
sand in their hair

and a dog comes too.